THERE WAS AN OLD LADY WHO SWALLOWED A BAT!

by Lucille Colandro

Illustrated by Jared Lee

SCHOLASTIC INC.

New York Toronto London Auckland Sydney
Mexico City New Delhi Hong Kong Buenos Aires

To my favorite wizards — David and Gene
Love,
L.C.

To my daughter Jana
who loves Halloween
— J.L.

ISBN-13: 978-0-545-16353-8
ISBN-10: 0-545-16353-6

10 9 8 7 6 5 4 3 2 1 9 10 11 12 13 14/0

Printed in China
This edition first printing, September 2009

There was an old lady
who swallowed a bat.
I don't know why she swallowed a bat,
imagine that.

There was an old lady
who swallowed an owl.

My, oh, my, she started to howl.

She swallowed the owl to shush the bat.
I don't know why she swallowed a bat,
imagine that.

There was an old lady
who swallowed a cat.
What do you think? Now she's so fat.

She swallowed the cat to chase the owl.

She swallowed the owl to shush the bat.
I don't know why she swallowed a bat,
imagine that.

There was an old lady
who swallowed a ghost.
What do you think?

She liked it the most!

She swallowed the ghost to catch the cat.
She swallowed the cat to chase the owl.

She swallowed the owl to shush the bat.
I don't know why she swallowed a bat,
imagine that.

There was an old lady
who swallowed a goblin.

It made her so dizzy, she started to spin.

She swallowed the goblin

to scare the ghost.

She swallowed the ghost to catch the cat.

She swallowed the cat to chase the owl.

She swallowed the owl to shush the bat.
I don't know why she swallowed a bat,
imagine that.

There was an old lady
who swallowed some bones.

There were so many, she started to groan.

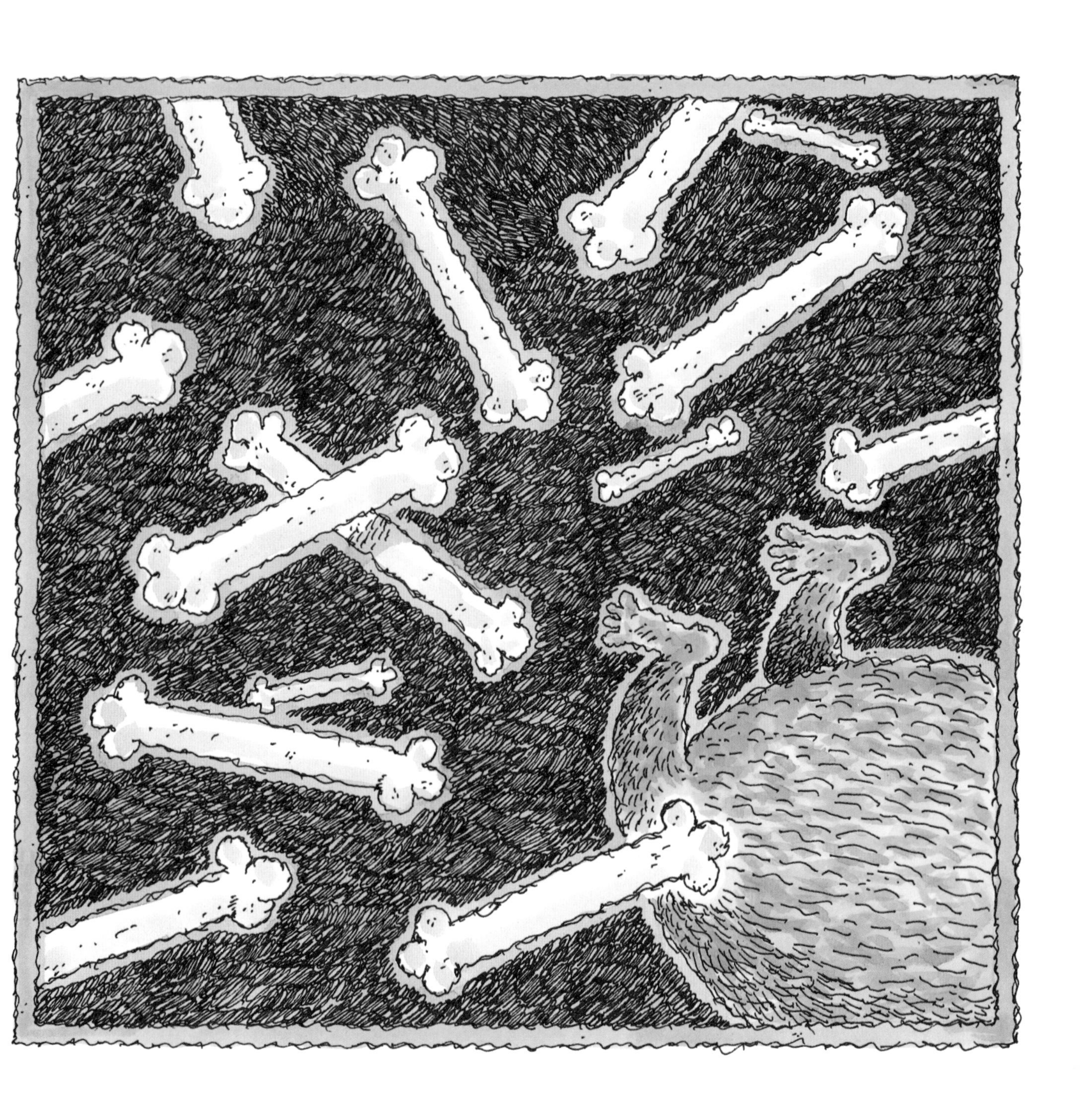

She swallowed the bones to rattle the goblin.

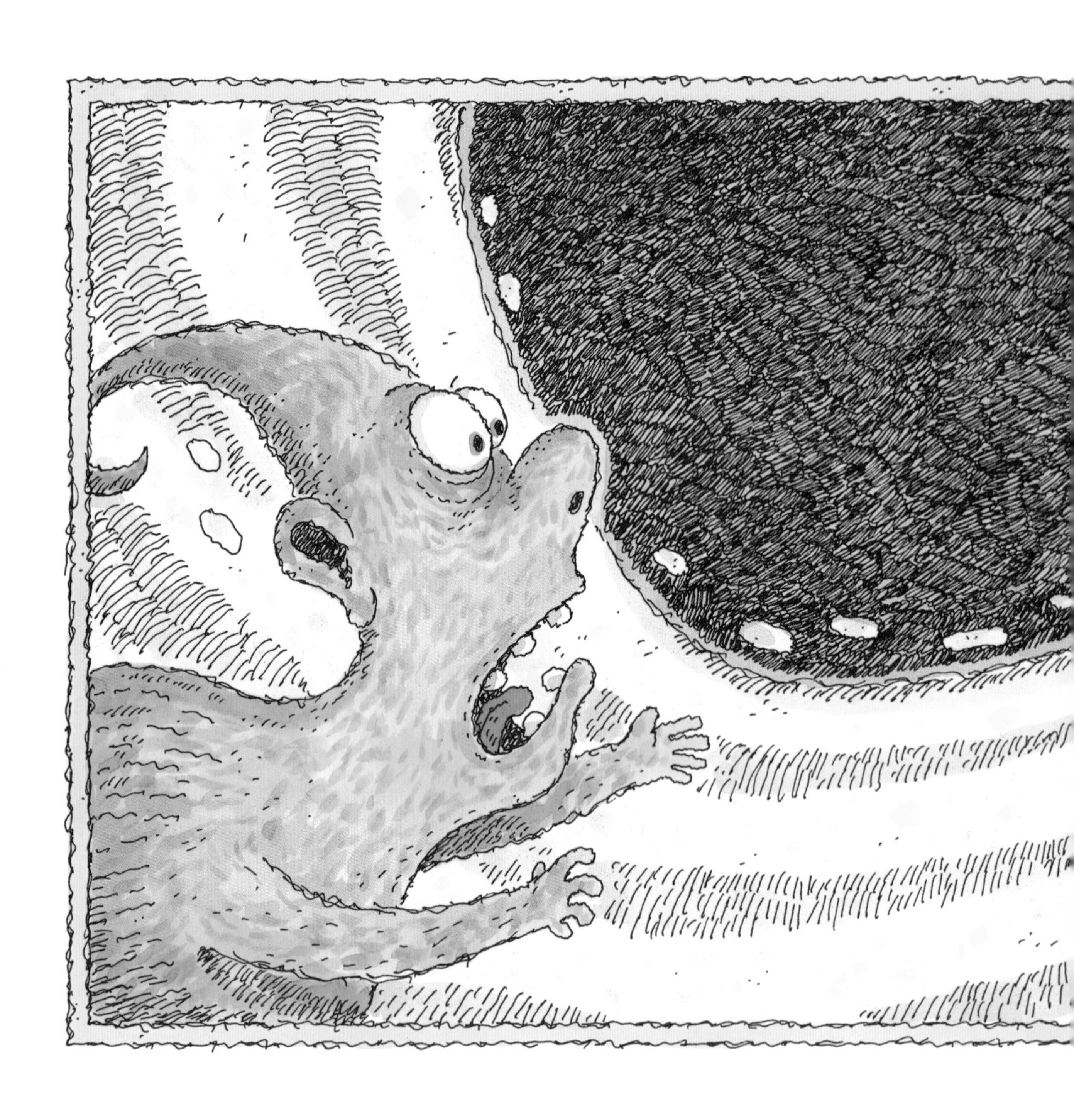

She swallowed the goblin to scare the ghost.

She swallowed the ghost to catch the cat.

She swallowed the cat to chase the owl.
She swallowed the owl to shush the bat.

I don't know why she swallowed a bat,
imagine that.

There was an old lady
who swallowed a wizard

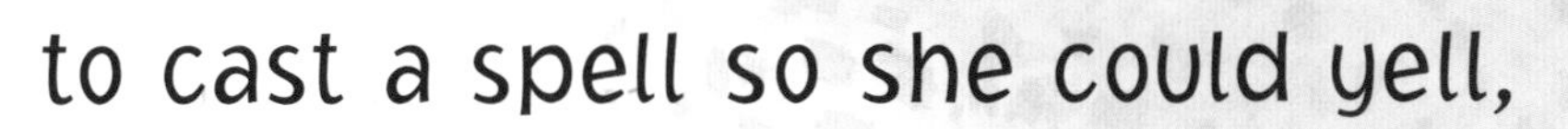

to cast a spell so she could yell,

“TRICK OR

TREAT!”

Burp!